Frosty the Snowman and the Magic Day

By Rita Balducci

Illustrated by Jean Chandler

A GOLDEN BOOK ▪ NEW YORK

Western Publishing Company, Inc., Racine, Wisconsin 53404

 Library of Congress Catalog Card Number: 90-85636
ISBN: 0-307-12339-1/ISBN: 0-307-62339-4 (lib. bdg.)

MCMXCIII

After a long and snowy winter, spring was coming. Buds appeared on all the trees. Robins came back to their nests. Each day it was getting warmer and the snow was melting fast. Frosty the Snowman knew the time had come for him to leave.

On his way, he stopped off to visit Mother Nature. She lived in a beautiful high cloud where Frosty would not melt. The snowman liked to visit her in the spring and watch her using her magic to make the sun shine brightly and the flowers grow.

Back on earth, Frosty's friend Mary was just getting better after a long illness which had kept her inside almost all winter. Now Mary wanted to go outside and play in the snow with her friends. Most of all, she wanted to play with her good friend Frosty the Snowman.

Finally, one bright and sunny morning, Mary's mother said, "I think what you need now is fresh air and sunshine. Do you want to go outside today?"

"Oh, boy!" Mary said excitedly. She jumped out of bed. "I can't wait to see Frosty!"

Mary danced up and down while her mother bundled her into her jacket and scarf.

"Keep your hat on!" Mary's mother called after her as she raced out the door. "Make sure you stay warm!"

Mary barely heard her mother. "Here I come!" she shouted, bounding down the back steps.

Mary soon found her friends. But Frosty was nowhere to be seen. "Where's Frosty?" Mary asked.

"Frosty couldn't stay any longer," Sarah said sadly.

"There's no snow left," Peter added. "It was getting too warm."

"But he'll be back next winter," said David, hoping to cheer Mary up.

"*Next* winter?!" Mary cried. "But I want to go ice skating! I want to throw snowballs! I wish there could be just one more snowy day so Frosty and I can play before he has to go away!" Then she sat down on her back steps and began to cry.

From high up in Mother Nature's cloud, Frosty saw Mary and heard her talking to her friends. When he realized how sad Mary was, Frosty decided to ask Mother Nature for a special favor.

"Please, Mother Nature," he said, "can we have one more snowy day? My friend Mary hasn't had a chance to go ice skating, or throw snowballs, or go sledding this winter. Just one day is all we need."

"Of course, Frosty," said Mother Nature. "But the snow clouds are a little sleepy after the long winter. You'll have to wake them up!"

So Frosty went back to Mary's house, where all the children were trying to cheer her up.

"Frosty!" Mary cried as soon as she saw him. "I thought I would have to wait a whole year before I saw you again! Aren't you going to melt?"

"Not today," Frosty replied. "Now, everyone hold hands. We're going to have one last day of winter!"

"Yay!" they all shouted as they grabbed each other's hands. Then they began to rise up into the air. Up, up, up they went!

"This is neat!" Peter said as they reached a fluffy white cloud.

"Okay, everybody let go!" Frosty said. So they all let go of each other's hands and—*POUF!*—landed in deep, soft, foamy snowdrifts.

The children ran and slid all over the little cloud. They threw snowballs. They jumped into snowdrifts. But not once did any of them feel cold. Frosty's magic kept them all as warm as can be!

"I think this cloud is asleep," Frosty said. "We're going to have to tickle it so that it wakes up and starts to snow for us."

So they all began to tickle the cloud. (They tickled each other a little bit, too!)

Before long the little cloud began to shake. Then it began to giggle softly. Soon it was laughing and shaking and wiggling all at once.

"Hey, look!" Mary said, pointing. "It's starting to snow!"

"Grab yourself a snowflake," shouted Frosty as he climbed onto a large one passing by.

Mary jumped up and grabbed onto a great big snowflake. "Whee!" she cried as she started floating back to earth.

Soon every child was riding a snowflake. They held on tight and softly floated back to earth.

"LOOK OUT BELOW!" Frosty shouted as his snowflake spun in circles.

"Whee!" cried all the children as the wind twirled them round in the sky.

Such big snowflakes covered the countryside quickly in a blanket of white. Now everyone came out of their houses to watch as the children floated gently down to the ground.

Mary's mother called out, "Mary! Are you sure you're warm enough?"

"Yes, Mom." Mary giggled as her snowflake landed in a field.

Every child in town was running and playing in the newly fallen snow.

"Hurray for Frosty's present!" they all shouted. "We are having one more day of winter after all!"

That night they all went for a sleigh ride.
As they rode, the children sang:

"Hurray for Frosty!
He saved the day
By making it snow
So that we could play.
Three cheers for Frosty—
Jump in the sleigh—
Hurray! Hurray! Hurray!"